THIS CANDLEWICK BOOK BELONGS TO:

_____

_____

_____

_____

To the Underwoods

Copyright © 1989 by Charlotte Voake

First U.S. paperback edition 1997

Library of Congress Cataloging-in-Publication Data
Voake, Charlotte.
Mrs. Goose's baby / Charlotte Voake. — 1st U.S. paperback ed.
Summary: Mrs. Goose is a devoted mother to her new baby but
is puzzled by the baby's strange behavior.
ISBN 0-7636-0092-X
[1. Geese — Fiction. 2. Mother and child — Fiction.] I. Title.
[PZ7.V855Mr 1997]
[E] — dc20   96-8417

2 4 6 8 10 9 7 5 3

Printed in Hong Kong

This book was hand lettered by Charlotte Voake.
The pictures were done in watercolor and ink.

Candlewick Press
2067 Massachusetts Avenue
Cambridge, Massachusetts 02140

Mrs.
Goose's
Baby

Charlotte Voake

CANDLEWICK PRESS
CAMBRIDGE, MASSACHUSETTS

One day Mrs. Goose found an egg

and made a nest to put it in.

She sat on the egg

to keep it safe and warm.

Soon the egg started to crack open.

The little bird inside was
pecking at the shell.

Mrs. Goose's baby was very small.
She was fluffy and yellow.

Mrs. Goose took her baby out
to eat some grass.

But her baby didn't want to eat grass.
She ran off to look for
something different.

Mrs. Goose took her baby to the pond
to teach her how to swim.

But her baby just sat on the shore.

 Mrs. Goose's baby grew

and grew

and grew.

Mrs. Goose's feathers were smooth and white.

Her baby's feathers were brown.
They weren't smooth at all.

Mrs. Goose had large webbed feet.
Her baby had little
pointy toes.

The baby followed Mrs. Goose everywhere
and cuddled up to her at night.

Mrs. Goose loved her baby very much and kept her safe from strangers.

Mrs. Goose's baby never did
eat much grass.

HONK!

She never did go swimming
in the pond.

And everyone except Mrs. Goose knew why.

Mrs. Goose's baby was a

CHICKEN!

CHARLOTTE VOAKE's illustrations are widely loved for their gentle wit. She says, "I don't know that I'm a funny person. But it seems when I begin to draw that the characters change and they take on this amusing and amused look." Charlotte Voake is the author-illustrator of *Mr. Davies and the Baby* as well as the illustrator of *Over the Moon*, a collection of nursery rhymes, *The Three Little Pigs and Other Favorite Nursery Stories*, and *Caterpillar Caterpillar* by Vivian French.

LAKE COUNTY PUBLIC LIBRARY
INDIANA

THIS BOOK IS RENEWABLE BY PHONE OR IN PERSON IF THERE IS NO RESERVE
WAITING OR FINE DUE.

LCP #0390